D1195474

HARLEY

Star Livingstone

Illustrated by Molly Bang

SeaStar Books
NEW YORK

To Sue and Emmy,
and Jeff
   —S. L. and M. B.

Text copyright © 2001 by Star Livingstone
Illustrations copyright © 2001 by Molly Bang

SEASTAR BOOKS
A division of NORTH-SOUTH BOOKS INC.

First published in the United States by SeaStar Books, a division of North-South Books Inc.,
New York. Published simultaneously in Canada, Australia, and New Zealand by
North-South Books, an imprint of Nord-Süd Verlag AG, Gossau Zürich, Switzerland.

Library of Congress Cataloging-in-Publication Data
Livingstone, Star.
Harley / Star Livingstone; illustrated by Molly Bang.
     p.   cm.
Summary: Because Harley the llama does not get along with other llamas, he becomes a
guard llama, protecting sheep from hungry coyotes and befriending a cantankerous ram.
[1. Llamas—Fiction. 2. Sheep—Fiction.]   I. Bang, Molly, ill. II. Title.
PZ7.L762 Har 2001   [E]—dc21   00-10434

ISBN 1-58717-048-5 (trade binding)
TB 10 9 8 7 6 5 4 3 2 1
ISBN 1-58717-049-3 (library binding)
LB 10 9 8 7 6 5 4 3 2 1

Printed by Proost NV in Belgium

For more information about our books, and the authors and artists who create them,
visit our web site: www.northsouth.com

Harley is a young llama.
He lives on a ranch.
He is learning to be a pack animal
and he is having a hard time.

He is supposed to wear a halter.

He wears a halter.

He does not like it.

He is supposed to wear a pack.

He wears a pack.

He does not like it.

He is supposed to follow people
down a path.

He would rather follow his own path.

He is supposed to get along
with other llamas.

He refuses.

When they come near, he screams.

He shoves.

He kicks.

He spits!

Today another llama comes too close.
Harley lays his ears way back.
He pulls his neck way back.
Then Harley spits.
He spits a long green gob straight
from his stomach.
It misses the llama.
It hits the teacher.

Splat!

It hits him right on the chin.

It drips down his shirt.

It smells awful.

Harley is in big trouble.

What will happen to Harley now?

A long way from the llama ranch
is a big field.
Rabbits and woodchucks live in it.
Turtles, mice, and crickets live in it too.
A fence runs around part of the field.
Sheep live inside the fence.

The sheep belong to the shepherd.

Every day she comes to care for them.

Every day she brings her dogs.

She is teaching the dogs

to herd sheep.

There are woods nearby.

Coyotes live in the woods.

It is winter now.

Rabbits are few.

The coyotes are hungry.

The sheep are fat and woolly.

They look good to the coyotes.

The fence looks easy to jump.

The coyotes feel brave.
Night comes.
There is a full moon.
The coyotes go hunting.
They go hunting sheep.

The shepherd comes in the morning.
She brings hay and grain.
She brings water.
She counts the sheep.
There is one missing.
She walks over the field looking.
She sees some wool.
Later, she finds a few bones.
That is all.
That is all that is left
of the missing sheep.
The coyotes were very hungry.

The shepherd knows coyotes.
She knows they will come back.
She makes the fence higher.
The coyotes do come again.
They jump the high fence.
They take a bigger sheep this time.
Again they eat it all.

The shepherd does not know
what to do.
She cannot keep the sheep safe.
She asks for help.
"Buy a gun."
"Put out poison."
"Get a guard llama."
"Don't get a llama."

"Trap the coyotes."

"Build a higher fence."

The shepherd listens to everyone.

She does not want to lose more sheep.

She does not want to kill the coyotes.

She has to do something soon.

She thinks a guard llama might work.

She thinks a llama might be fun.

She decides to try that.

The shepherd calls a llama ranch.
She tells the owner she needs
a guard llama.

The owner thinks she can help.

She has many llamas for sale.

The shepherd goes to the ranch.

She looks at llamas.

Some are too small.

Some don't like people.

Some are only happy with other llamas.

Many are trained
to be pack animals.

None of them are quite
what the shepherd wants.

The last llama is Harley.

The shepherd likes
the look of Harley.

She thinks he might like her field.

She hopes he will like her sheep.

She will take a chance on Harley.

Harley is in the back of the truck.

He has been there a long time.

The shepherd opens the tailgate.

She grabs the halter rope.

Harley scrambles out.

He stretches his front legs.

He stretches his back legs.

He is happy to walk around.

The shepherd opens the field gate.

Harley sees the sheep.

He runs through the gate.

He races toward the sheep.

The ram charges at Harley.

The sheep scatter in all directions.

Everyone is upset.

The shepherd is worried.

She is afraid she made a mistake.

Too late now.

She must wait and see.

In the morning the shepherd returns.

Everything is settled.

Harley is guarding the sheep.

They are his sheep now.

The field is his field.

What happened?

Only Harley and the sheep know.

The shepherd brings Harley his own
helping of grain every morning.
She puts it on top of the small shed.
Harley can reach it
but the sheep cannot.
It is her way of telling him
that he is special.
Harley loves his treat.
He watches for the shepherd
every day.
He lets her come very near.
Sometimes he eats out of her hand.

In late winter, lambs are born.
The wind howls.
The snow blows.
It is very cold.

The shepherd puts clean straw
in the sheep shed.
She hangs a light there.
She brings in the mother sheep.
The lambs are born in the shed.
They are safe from the wind and cold.

Harley wants to be with the lambs.

He wants to stay with the mothers.

Harley wants to be with the flock too.

He does not want to leave them alone.

He runs back and forth.

Now he is in the shed.

Now he is in the field.

He hums.

He cannot decide.

The shepherd helps him.

She shuts the gate in between.

Harley loves the lambs.

He touches each one with his nose.

He wants to be sure none are missing.

By spring the lambs are growing fast.

They run and jump all day.

One climbs on his mother's back.

The others try to push him off.

The mothers do not seem to mind.

They lie still and chew.

The lambs try to play their game
on Harley.
Harley *does* mind.
He lays his ears back flat.
He stands up.
The lambs fall off.
Harley goes somewhere else
to lie down.
The lambs just try again.
Too many lambs for Harley!

The ram is the biggest sheep
in the field.

He pushes and shoves.

He butts everyone.

The ewes do not like him.

They turn their backs.

The lambs do not like him.

They keep out of his way.

The dogs do not like him.

They nip his heels.

The shepherd puts a bell
around his neck.

Now he cannot sneak up on her.

She feels sorry for the ewes and lambs.

She often feeds them
in a different pen.

She leaves the ram with Harley.

She thinks Harley can take care
of himself.

One day the shepherd comes
to check on the sheep.
There they are, eating grass.
There is Harley, lying down.
There is the ram, next to Harley.
He is standing very close.

He leans on Harley.
Harley turns his head.
He touches the ram's nose
with his nose.
The ram rubs his head
on Harley's neck.
The shepherd watches.

The ram backs away.

He shakes his head from side to side.

He stands still.

Then he charges at Harley.

Harley watches him coming.

The ram comes nearer and nearer.

Harley gets up.

He gets up just in time.

Up go his front legs.

The ram runs right under him.

Harley lies down again.

The ram returns.

He stands next to Harley.

They touch noses.

GOOD GAME!

It is a dark night.
Three coyotes go hunting.
"Yip, yip, yip!"
they call.

The sheep are restless.
They crowd together.
The coyotes sound close.
They ARE close.
They run along the fence.
They look for a good place
to jump over.
They find one.

Suddenly there is a loud noise
inside the fence.
Harley is screaming.
Harley is running.
His legs fly out every which way.
His neck waves back and forth.

Harley runs from the sheep to the fence.
The coyotes are not there.

They have run away.

They will hunt somewhere else tonight.

"Baa! Baa! Baa!"

There is a lot of noise in the hay barn.

The whole flock is in there.

Harley is there too.

Today is shearing day.

Today the sheep lose their coats.

The shearer grabs a sheep.

She flips it onto its back.

The sheep gets quiet.

The clippers peel off the wool.

It all comes off in one piece.

The shepherd bundles it into a bag.

"Next!" calls the shearer.

Harley is the last.

He has never been sheared before.

He is not sure he likes the clippers.

He lets the shepherd hold him.

He lets the shearer clip him.

His wool is thick and soft.

He has lots of it.

The shepherd enters the best sheep
fleeces in the county fair.
This year she will enter
a llama fleece too.
When the shearing is done,
there is a big pile of wool in bags.
The sheep look smaller.
Their legs look longer.
They feel funny without their coats.
This is a big change.
They are a little scared.
Later on they will be glad.
They will be cool all summer.
Their coats will grow back
before winter.

The shepherd has a new dog.

Her name is Jet.

Jet knows how to herd cows.

She is afraid of cows.

Jet knows how to herd sheep.

She is not afraid of sheep.

She does a good job with them.

The shepherd sends Jet into
the sheep pen.

Harley sees
her coming.

Harley does not know Jet.

He sees a strange dog.

He sees it coming after his sheep.

Harley charges.

He chases Jet.

Jet runs to the shepherd.

She has never seen a llama before.
Now she is afraid of cows and llamas.

The shepherd lets the sheep out.
She shuts Harley in.
She tells Jet where to move the sheep.
Harley watches.
He hums.
He is not sure his sheep
are safe with Jet.
He will get used to her
after a while.

One day the shepherd comes
bringing Harley a treat.
She has grain and apple peels
in a bowl.
She holds the bowl over the fence.
Harley runs over.
He starts to gobble up the food.
The ram wants some too.

He pokes the bottom of the bowl
with his nose.
Harley gulps the food faster.
The ram squeezes up to the fence.
Harley makes gurgly warning noises.
Finally the ram backs away.
Harley is eating as fast as he can.

The ram runs up and butts Harley.

Harley turns in a flash.

He spits hard.

His mouth is full of grain.

It sprays all over the ram.

The ram stops short.
Harley stops too.
They look at each other.
They look at the grain on the ground.
Then they both eat.

It is HOT.

It has been hot for days.

It is too hot for Harley.

He digs and rolls in the dirt.

He shows his teeth.

He hums.

He lets the sheep wander off.

He does not go after them.

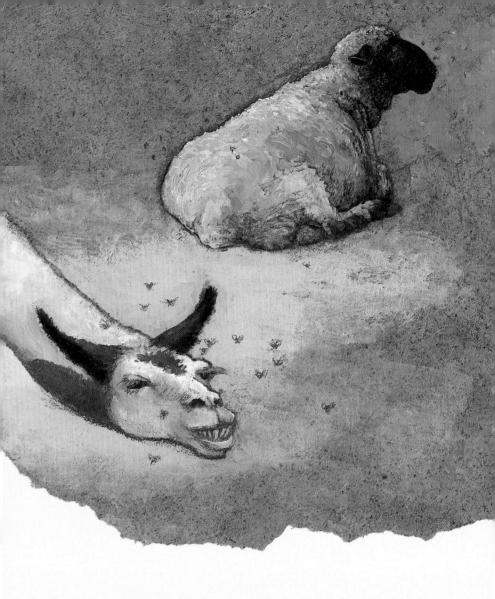

The summer heat goes on.

The grass dries up.

Dust and flies are thick.

The shepherd brings a wading pool.

She brings water barrels.

Then she turns on a hose.

Harley runs over to watch.

The shepherd points the hose
at Harley.

He steps closer.

He turns this way and that.

He seems to say,

"Spray my back."

"Spray my chin."

"Spray my legs."

"More on my neck."

"Aah, that feels good!"

The next day the shepherd
comes again.
She comes to fill the water barrels.
She sends the dogs to fetch the sheep.
All the sheep come running.
They come running to drink.
Harley sees the shepherd.
He sees the water
but he does not come close.
What is wrong?

After a while another sheep
comes over the hill.
She was left behind.
Harley was waiting for her.
He runs now.
He runs up behind the sheep.
He gives her a big push.
He shoves her toward the shepherd.
Now Harley can come for his shower.
Now he can get cool.

Today the shepherd has sold
two sheep.
Two strangers load the sheep
into their truck.
Harley is close by.
He is in the way.
He does not want his sheep to go.
The truck drives off.
Harley follows as far as he can.
He follows to the corner
of the fence.
He watches the truck go
out of sight.
He knows those sheep
will not be back.
Harley runs to the middle
of the field.

He throws himself down.

He rolls and rolls on his back.

His legs wave around in the air.

He hums and shows his teeth.

Harley is having a tantrum.

After a while he stops.

He gets up and walks over to the flock.

He lies down among his sheep.

The shepherd has been thinking
about getting a new ram.
Now somebody wants to buy her ram.
She thinks about this on the way
to the county fair.
Sheep judging is today.
The shepherd is excited.
She goes to the wool barn first.

She sees that Harley's fleece
has won a blue ribbon.
It is for
BEST RARE AND UNUSUAL ANIMAL.
People who spin wool into yarn
want to buy Harley's fleece.
The shepherd is proud of Harley
and his prize.

Now she looks at the sheep fleeces.
Who has won first place?
It is the ram.
He has a blue ribbon too!
She begins to think about the ram.
He has prize wool.
He is strong.
His lambs are strong lambs.
He and Harley are friends.
He has not been as mean
since Harley came.
The shepherd thinks she has
a good ram already.
She thinks she will keep him
another year.

It is early morning.

The pen gate is open.

Harley is ready.

He keeps his neck very straight.

He holds his head up high.

He wears his ears like a crown.

He walks slowly.

He is leading his sheep out to pasture.

They follow in a long line.

At midday the sun is hot.

The path across the field is empty.

Sheep are scattered all over.

Some sleep.

Some graze.

The ram's bell rings as he eats.

A crow caws.

Harley rests on the hill.